WHY YOU NEED TO KNOW . . . PERIOD

Sonali Shenoy

Illustrations by
Annushka Hardikar

PUFFIN BOOKS
An imprint of Penguin Random House

PUFFIN BOOKS

USA | Canada | UK | Ireland | Australia
New Zealand | India | South Africa | China

Puffin Books is part of the Penguin Random House group of companies
whose addresses can be found at global.penguinrandomhouse.com

Published by Penguin Random House India Pvt. Ltd
4th Floor, Capital Tower 1, MG Road,
Gurugram 122 002, Haryana, India

First published in Puffin Books by Penguin Random House India 2021

10 9 8 7 6 5 4 3 2 1

This is a work of fiction. Names, characters, places and incidents are either the product of the author's imagination or are used fictitiously and any resemblance to any actual person, living or dead, events or locales is entirely coincidental.

ISBN 9780143451921

Book design and layout by Devangana Dash
Typeset in Agmena Pro and Action Man
Printed at Aarvee Promotions, India

www.penguin.co.in

To change,
to questions,
to growing up

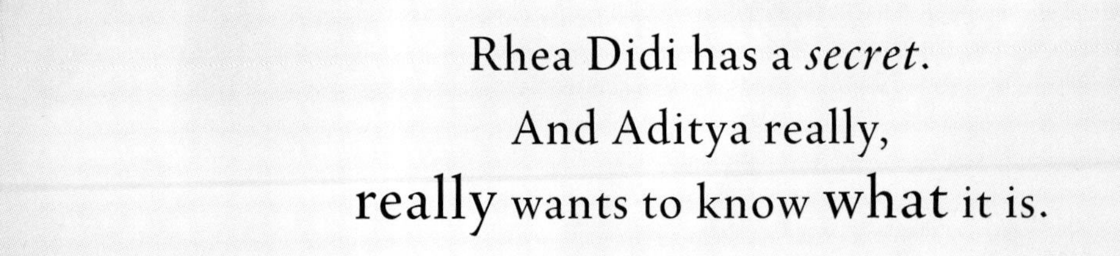

Rhea Didi has a *secret*.
And Aditya really,
really wants to know what it is.

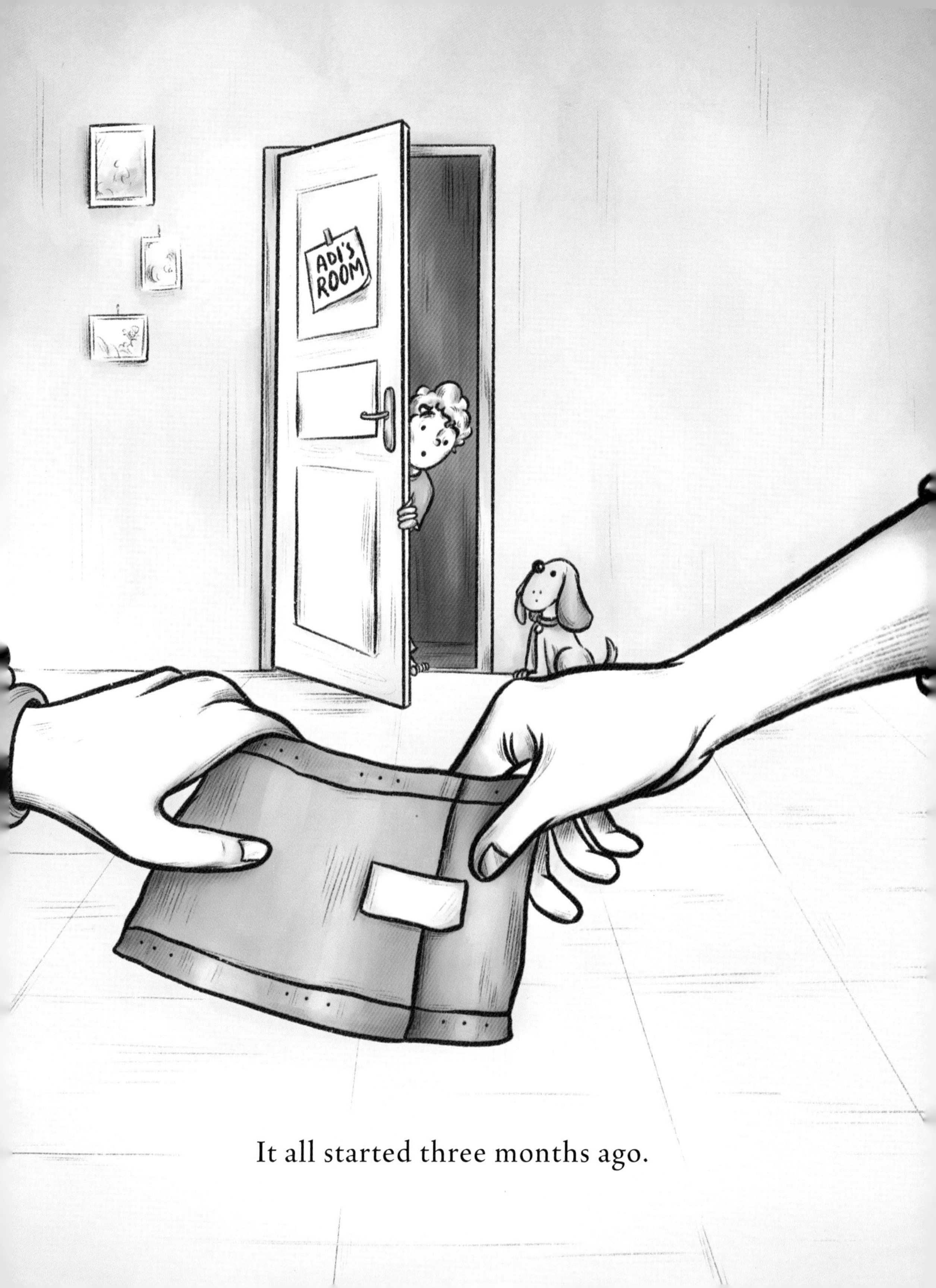

It all started three months ago.

Right after she came out of the bathroom and gave a scary, loud . . .
EEEEEEEEEE EEEEEEE!
'WHAT'S WRONG WITH DIDI?'
Aditya nearly fell out of his chair.
'IS SHE ALL RIGHT?'

Mama looked around sheepishly.
She suddenly seemed to have gone red.

**'DON'T WORRY YOUR LITTLE HEAD.
GET READY FOR SCHOOL NOW,'**
she said, sending him on his way.

But Aditya knew something was going on
that **no one** was telling him about.
And he was determined
to get to the bottom of it.

Aditya wanted presents to be **secretly** delivered to his room too . . . or erm, the bathroom!

After all, what could Rhea Didi have done to deserve a **gift**?

'PERIODS,' whispered Naveen.
His best friend usually had all the answers.

'NO, NO! NOT THAT PERIOD. THIS IS SOMETHING ONLY GIRLS HAVE. DON'T YOU KNOW?'
Naveen whispered with a giggle.

'THAT'S WHY THEY BUY THOSE . . . WHAT DO YOU CALL THEM?'

'WELL, DUH! WE ARE IN SCIENCE "PERIOD" RIGHT NOW.'
Aditya leaned forward, wide-eyed with curiosity.

'WHAT'S GOING ON HERE, BOYS? DO YOU WANT TO SHARE YOUR INTERESTING STORY WITH THE ENTIRE CLASS??'

Aditya blurted out the first thing that came to his mind.
UH, MA'AM. WH-WHAT ARE PERIODS?

WHAT NONSENSE!
ASK YOUR MOTHER.
NOW FOCUS ON THE LESSON
OR GET OUT OF MY CLASS!

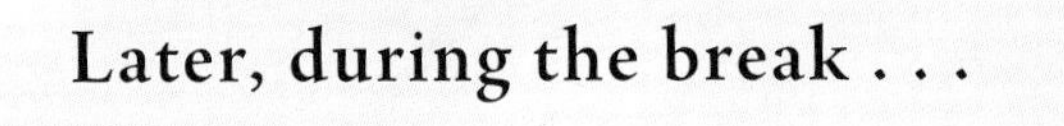

Later, during the break . . .

Vinay pulled something out of his bag and looked around to make sure no one was watching.

The three boys huddled around it with curiosity . . .
I GOT THIS FROM MY SISTER'S BAG WHEN SHE WASN'T LOOKING.

When suddenly . . .

WELL, IT ACTUALLY MAY BE! THAT'S WHY THE PACKAGING SAYS IT HAS WINGS!

SO, THIS IS A PERIOD? I THINK I'VE SEEN THIS ON TV IN THE ADS. THEY USE IT FOR INK, DON'T THEY? BUT WHY WOULD MY SISTER NEED IT? SHE USES A MICROTIP PEN.

'DADI, DO YOU NEED HELP
CUTTING THOSE VEGETABLES?'
Dadi smiled.
Aditya shifted in his seat.
SO I HAVE A QUESTION
FOR YOU, DADI. WHAT ARE . . .
PERIODS?

EH?! I'M A LITTLE BUSY, ADITYA.

Later, with the
pizza delivery boy . . .

'DO YOU HAVE EXTRA SAUCE PACKETS?

ALSO, WHAT ARE PERIODS?'

'GET INSIDE!' Mama yelled.

It seemed that no one wanted
to give Aditya the answer.
That night, just before he was about to sleep,
there was a knock on the door.
ADI, CAN I COME IN?

I . . . SAW TODAY THAT THERE WAS SOMETHING YOU REALLY, REALLY, REALLY WANTED TO KNOW.
WHAT'S THE POINT?
Aditya mumbled.
NO ONE WANTS TO TELL ME! SERIOUSLY, WHAT IS THE BIG DEAL?
BUT YOU NEVER ASKED . . . ME.
WE HAVEN'T TALKED SINCE YOU . . . STARTED KEEPING SECRETS. AND WHY ARE YOU GETTING PRESENTS IN THE BATHROOM?

I WAS JUST TAKING SOME TIME
TO GET USED TO . . . A CHANGE.
BUT I WOULDN'T KEEP A SECRET FROM YOU.
YOU'RE MY BROTHER.

This made Aditya feel a wee bit better.
And he decided to ask his question out loud
one last time.

SO WHEN A GIRL REACHES A CERTAIN AGE,
SHE GETS A PERIOD.

BUT MAYBE DON'T GO ASKING YOUR FRIENDS
ABOUT IT, ESPECIALLY GIRLS. IT'S NEW AND
TAKES SOME GETTING USED TO. AND SO, THEY
MIGHT BE A BIT UNCOMFORTABLE TALKING
ABOUT IT.

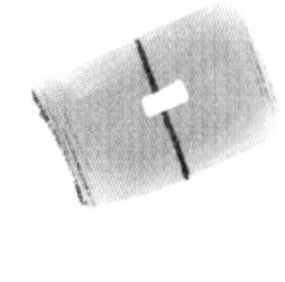

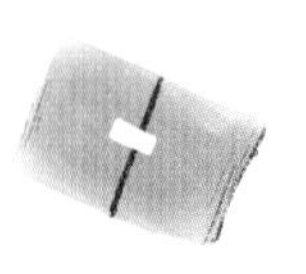

WAIT—SO PADS ARE NOT FOR SOAKING INK,
LIKE IN THE ADS?

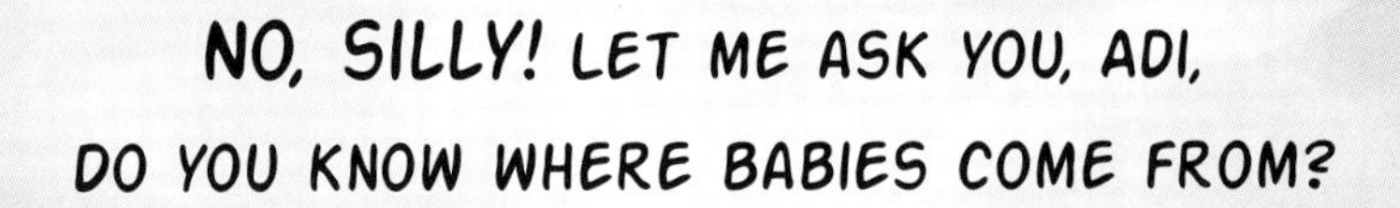

I CAME FROM MAMA'S TUMMY.

EXACTLY. AND BEFORE YOU ARRIVED, MAMA'S TUMMY CREATED A PILLOW FOR YOU TO SLEEP ON SO YOU COULD BE MORE COMFORTABLE.

Z Z Z Z

I LIKE PILLOWS.

EXCEPT THIS PILLOW WAS MADE OF THE MOST NUTRITIOUS INGREDIENTS IN THE WHOLE BODY FOR YOU TO BE HEALTHY AND STRONG . . . BLOOD.

BLOOD?? EWWWWWW!

SO, EVERY MONTH THAT CUSHION OF BLOOD GETS RELEASED IF THERE IS NO BABY TO SLEEP ON IT.
AND THAT IS WHAT A PERIOD IS.

NOW I AM USED TO IT. I JUST TELL MYSELF THAT IT'S PART OF WHO I AM. IT'S PART OF BEING A GIRL.
OKAY, NOW MY TURN, ADI. WHAT ARE YOU GOING TO DO, NOW THAT YOU KNOW WHAT A PERIOD IS?
UM, I JUST WANTED TO KNOW WHY I WAS BEING LEFT OUT. THANKS FOR TELLING ME, DIDI.

Two months later . . .
RHEA, FOR YOU.
WHAT, NO QUESTIONS, ADI?
IT LOOKS SMALLER THAN YOUR USUAL PACKAGE.
THAT'S BECAUSE . . . SHALL WE TELL HIM, MA?
YOU STARTED THIS. YOU FINISH IT.

WELL, ADI, I FOUND OUT RECENTLY THERE IS MORE THAN ONE WAY TO HANDLE MY PERIOD.
LYING DOWN TILL THE TUMMY PAIN GOES AWAY?
SWEET BOY. YES! THAT . . . AND TAMPONS.

And of course, this meant the start of a brand-new adventure.

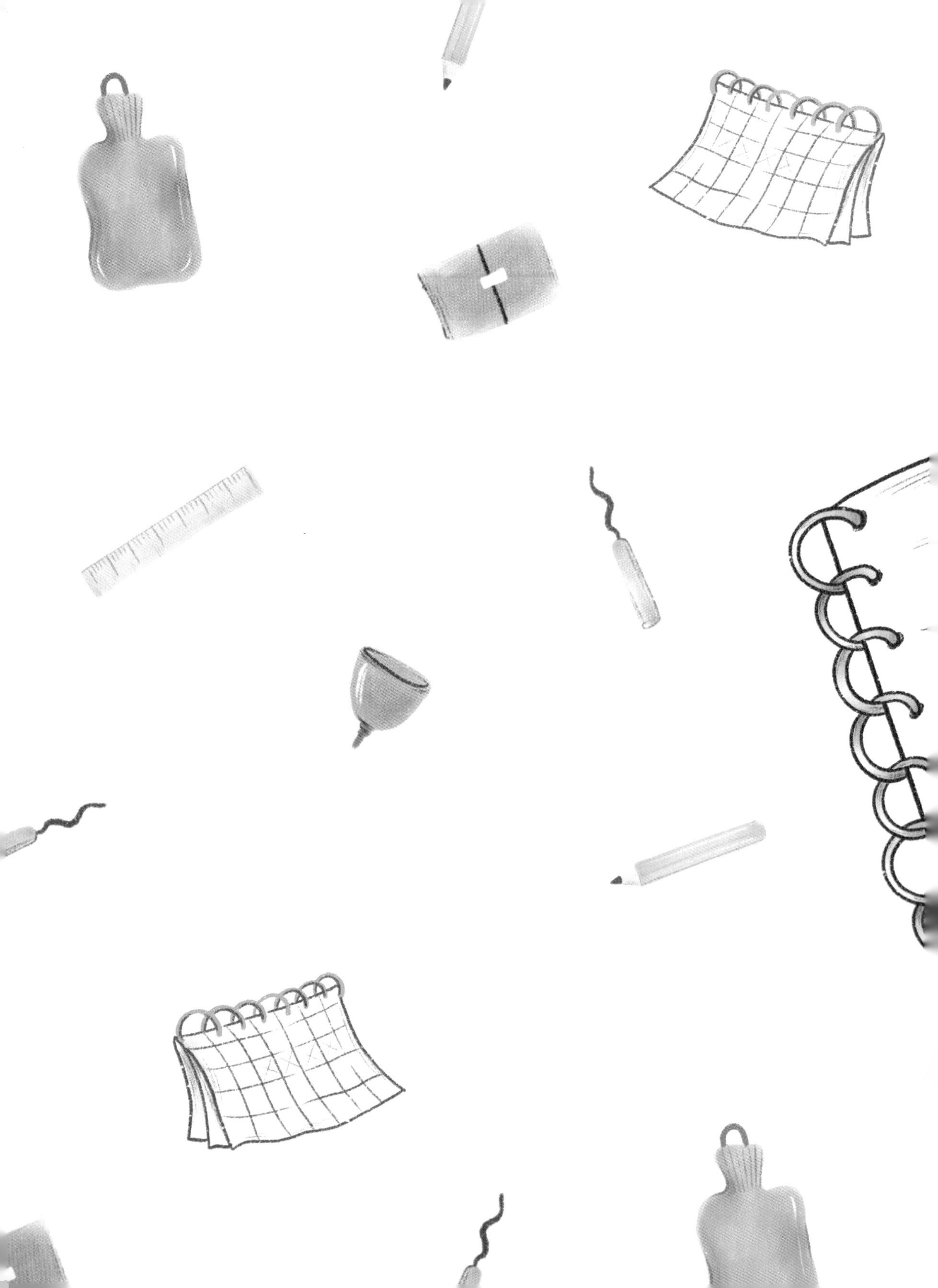

GLOSSARY
(WORDS YOU MIGHT HEAR GIRLS SAY)

MENSTRUATION

AUNT FLO

CHUMS/CHUMMING

SANITARY PAD

TAMPON

CRAMPS

MENSES

THAT TIME OF THE MONTH

LADY BUSINESS

SONALI SHENOY likes to seek out novel points of view. It's how she weaves mini adventures into the pages of her days. So, it's definitely a perk that her day job as a journalist has led her to meet all sorts of fun, interesting, famous and quirky people. Over the past decade at the *New Indian Express*, she's interviewed plenty of big names—from Shah Rukh Khan to Sunny Leone to Sadhguru. The latest in her treasure trove of Q and A rollercoasters was with Oscar winner Matthew McConaughey. When she isn't brewing up a new story, she can be found sipping a warm brew of chai. Puns, hugs and chocolates are a few of her favourite things.

ANNUSHKA HARDIKAR is somebody who likes to draw and occasionally gets paid for it. A storyteller at heart, she likes working on a variety of projects inspired by human psychology, gender, representation, her travels and documenting the magic in the mundane. Alongside working on commercial art projects, Annushka is the co-founder of A Fresh Coat, a project that aims to share stories of people and places through street art. A two-time TEDx speaker, she also enjoys public speaking and sharing honest creative journeys through her YouTube channel. You can find her on most days staring at trees, talking to dogs and scribbling away in her journal.